Goldilocks
and the
Three Bears

Adapted by Gina Kim

Illustrated by Y. K. Kim

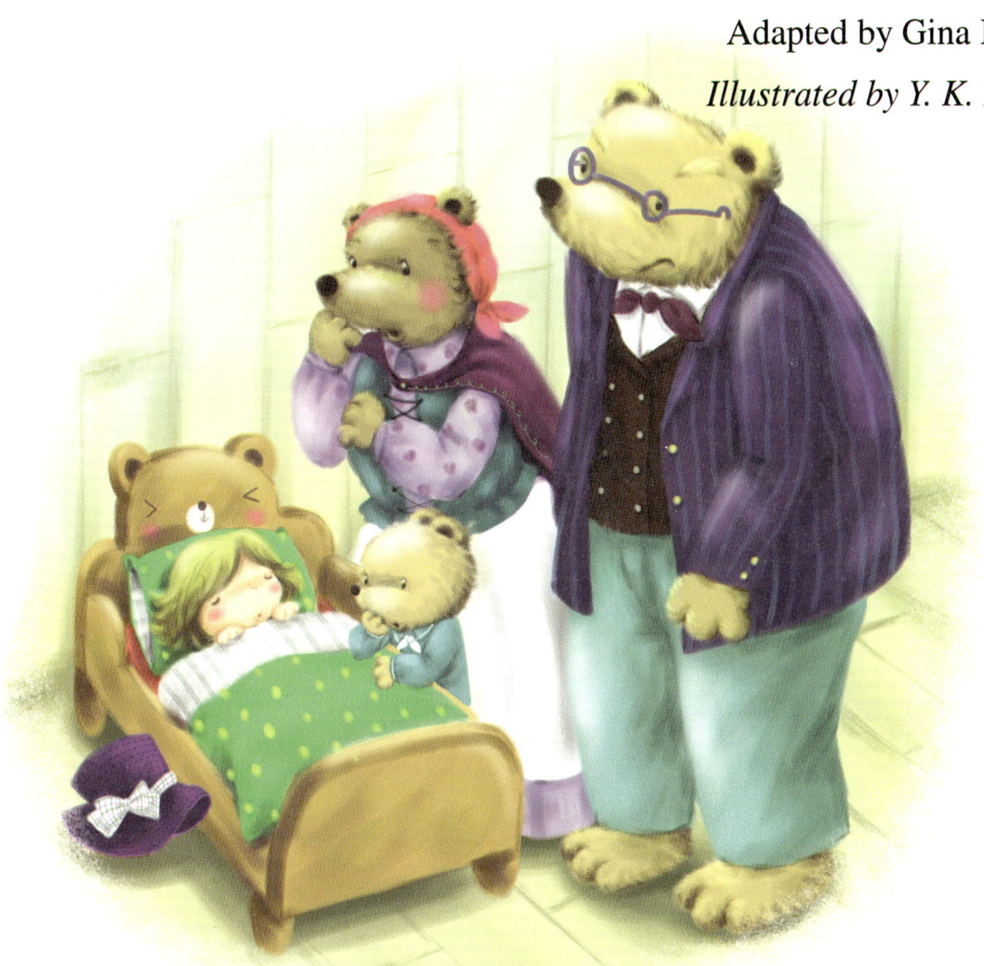

WorldCom ELT

This is the story of Goldilocks and three bears.
Goldilocks is a little girl.
She lives with her mother.

2

One day her mother says,  "Goldilocks,
go to the store. Buy two muffins and
some bread."
Goldilocks says, "OK."

Her mother says, "Be careful. Don't
go through the forest."
But Goldilocks walks through the forest.
She isn't afraid.

The three bears live
in a little house in
the forest:
Father bear,
Mother bear,
and Baby bear.

In the bears' house, there are three
chairs: a big chair for Father bear,
a smaller chair for Mother bear,
and a little chair for Baby bear.

There are three bowls on the table:
a big bowl for Father bear,
a smaller bowl for Mother bear,
and a little bowl for Baby bear.

There are three beds in the bedroom:
a big bed for Father bear,
a smaller bed for Mother bear,
and a little bed for Baby bear.

The three bears sit at the table.
They eat the porridge.
The porridge is too hot.
Father bear says,  "This porridge is
    hot!"

Mother bear says, "The porridge is
    too hot. We can't eat it now. Let's go for
    a walk."
So the three bears go for a walk in the
    forest.

Goldilocks walks through the forest.
She walks and walks.
She sees a house.

This is the bears' house.

She knocks on the door.
"Knock, knock."
She opens the door.

She says,  "Hello. Is anyone
  home?"
No one is home.

She sees three bowls of porridge
  on the table.

She eats the porridge in the big bowl.

She says, "Too hot!"

She eats the porridge in the smaller bowl.

She says, "Too cold!"

She eats the porridge in the little bowl.

She says, "Just right!"

So she eats the porridge in the little bowl.

Goldilocks sees three chairs.
She sits in the big chair.
She says, "Too hard!"
She sits in the smaller chair.
She says, "Too soft!"

She sits in the little chair.
She says, "Just right!"
But Goldilocks is bigger than Baby bear.
And the chair breaks.

Goldilocks is tired.
She walks up the stairs.
She sees three beds.
She sleeps in the big bed.
She says, "Too high!"
She sleeps in the smaller bed.
She says, "Still too high!"
She sleeps in the little bed.
She says, "Just right!"

Just then the three bears come home.
The little bowl is empty.
Baby bear says,  "My porridge! My
  bowl is empty!"
Baby bear is angry.

The three bears
see the chairs.
The chairs are
on the floor.

Baby bear says, "Where is my chair?
Look! It is broken!"
Baby bear sees his broken chair.
And he begins to cry.

The three bears go upstairs.
Baby bear says,  "Somebody is in my
  bed!"
Father bear says, "Who are you?"

Goldilocks wakes up.
She sees the three bears:
Father bear,
Mother bear,
and Baby bear.

Goldilocks is afraid.
She gets up quickly.
Goldilocks says, "I am sorry."

Father bear says, "Don't be afraid.
 We don't want to eat you."
Goldilocks jumps out of bed.

Baby bear says,  "Come back and play
with me."
But Goldilocks runs all the way home.
The three bears never see Goldilocks
again.

Mother bear makes new porridge for
  Baby bear.
Father bear makes a new chair for
  Baby bear.

Baby bear is happy.
He is happy to have new porridge.
He is happy to have a new chair.

Exercises

A. What is it?

1. It's a g<u>i r l</u>.

2. It's a b_ _ _.

3. It's a b_ _.

4. It's a c_ _ _ _.

5. It's a h_ _ _ _.

6. It's a s_ _ _ _.

B. Look at the picture.
Answer the questions. Yes or No?

1. Is she tall? ☐ Yes ✓ No

2. Is she little? ☐ Yes ☐ No

3. Are there three bowls of porridge? ☐ Yes ☐ No

4. Does she eat the porridge? ☐ Yes ☐ No

5. Does she eat the porridge in the little bowl first? ☐ Yes ☐ No

6. Is the porridge in the little bowl just right for her? ☐ Yes ☐ No

Glossary

bear

broken

bedroom

chair

bread

empty

girl

porridge

house

store

mother

table

Easy Story House

Beginner 1 (100 Words)
The Rich Man and the Shoemaker
Three Billy Goats
Thumbelina
Goldilocks and the Three Bears

Beginner 2 (150 Words)
Rumpelstiltskin
The Bremen Town Musicians
The Three Spinners
The Wonderful Musician

Elementary 1 (200 Words)
Henny Penny
The Velveteen Rabbit
The Five Brothers
The Three Little Men in the Woods

Story House

Beginner 1 (400 Words)
Snow White and The Seven Dwarves
Cinderella
The Ugly Duckling
Little Red Riding Hood

Beginner 2 (450 Words)
The Three Little Pigs
Puss in Boots
The Golden Goose
The Emperor's New Clothes

Goldilocks and the Three Bears

Gina Kim

© 2005 published by WorldCom Publishing Inc.

Cover/Interior Design : Graphic Communications E30
Illustrations : Y. K. Kim

ISBN : 89-8127-889-X

Desk Copy Request / Information
To place your desk copy request or for more information,
please contact the following office:
Tel : (02) 3273-4300   Fax : (02) 3273-4303